TURTLE and TORTOISE
Are NOT Friends

BY MIKE REISS • ILLUSTRATED BY ASHLEY SPIRES

HARPER
An Imprint of HarperCollinsPublishers

For David Copperfield —M.R.

For Ronya and her pant-less painter, Helena —A.S.

There is a place far, far away, and in that place two eggs found themselves in the same pen.

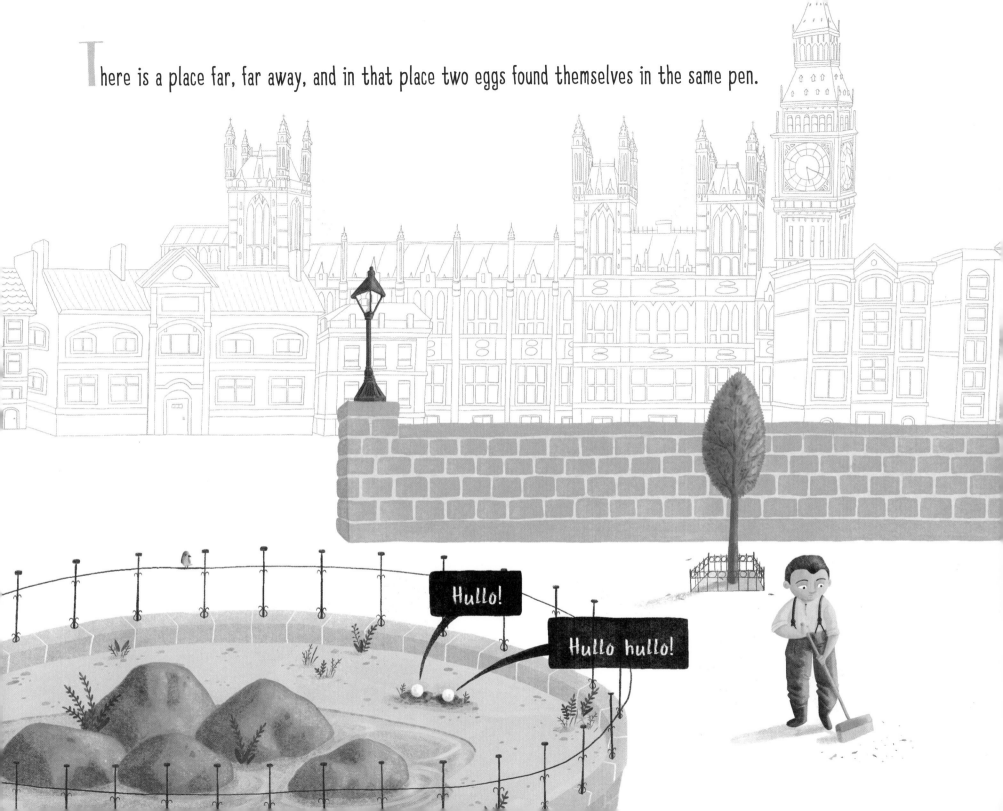

A turtle popped out of one egg.

A tortoise popped out of the other.

"What fun we'll have together!" said the turtle.
"We shall be best friends!" said the tortoise.
"People will call us the Terrible Turtle Twins!"

"Oh, but I'm not a turtle," said the tortoise, not quite so warmly. "I'm a tortoise. A turtle is a horrid beast with rough skin and a hard shell, while I am a handsome creature with a hard shell and rough skin."

"I understand," said the turtle, even though he didn't. "I guess we can't be friends."

"It just wouldn't make sense," said the tortoise.

And so the turtle and the tortoise walked to opposite sides of the pen.

Just then the zookeeper came by with a group of schoolchildren.
"In here we have a turtle and a tortoise. They can live to be one
hundred years old!"

Good heavens!

OVER THE NEXT FOURTEEN YEARS, the turtle and the tortoise had many interesting adventures. But each refused to tell the other about them.

The turtle found a worm that looked just like Winston Churchill.

He ate it.

Then another eagle carried him right back.

The tortoise was carried off by an eagle.

They went through some terrible winters . . .